Christmas
2005
My dearest Sophie,

Always remember:
Friendship is bigger
than fear.
All my love,
Mama

Sophie and the Sea Monster

Don Gillmor
Michael Martchenko

North Winds Press

An imprint of Scholastic Canada Ltd.

For Cormac, the bold explorer
— D.G.

To all the moondancers
— M.M.

The illustrations in this book were painted
in watercolour and gouache on Crescent Illustration Board.
The type is set in 18pt Bookman Old Style.

Library and Archives Canada Cataloguing in Publication

Gillmor, Don
Sophie and the sea monster / Don Gillmor ; illustrated
by Michael Martchenko.

ISBN 0-439-97461-5

I. Martchenko, Michael II. Title.

PS8563.I59S66 2005   jC813'.54   C2005-901402-4

6 5 4 3 2 1   Printed in Canada   05 06 07 08

Sophie worried about wearing the right clothes to school. She worried about big dogs, bats, thunderstorms, snapping turtles, and losing her homework.

She wondered what held the moon up and she worried that it would fall on her house. She worried about everything all the time. But most of all, Sophie worried that there was a sea monster under her bed.

At dinner, her brother Chester said, "I heard a sea monster under your bed last night, Sophie. A big one."

"*What?*" said Sophie.

"There's no such thing as a sea monster," said her mother.

"Chester's a sea monster," said her father.

That night, Sophie sat on her bed for two hours, trying to make herself brave. Finally, she looked under the bed.

There *was* a sea monster under her bed. He was blue, and smaller than she had expected.

"*Aaahhh!*" Sophie screamed. "There's a sea monster under my bed!"

"Not just under your bed," the sea monster said. "There are sea monsters *everywhere*."

*H*e began to sing.

Oh, we're scandalously scaly,
a bit inclined to drool
We lie beneath your bed
and in the deep end of the pool
We may be long and wonderful
or maybe short and weird
We might be shy and humorous,
perhaps we have a beard

6

We could be tall and pimply
or sad and blue or simply
fabulous and dishy
or red and really squishy
or brown and mean
and rarely seen,
and nicely dressed
(though hardly clean)
with heads that look like lima beans
and teeth that seem a little blue
from brushing with your new shampooooo...

*A*s the sea monster sang his song, Sophie stared at him. He wasn't very scary, she thought. He wasn't a great singer either.

"Why are you under my bed?" Sophie asked.

"I like it here," said the sea monster.

"What do you eat?" Sophie asked.

"Socks mostly," he said. "One from each pair."

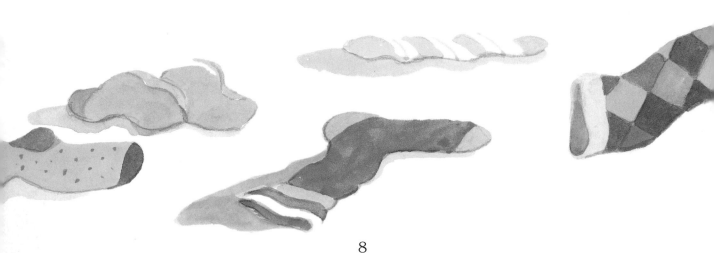

Sophie didn't really want a sea monster under her bed. She tried to pull him out but he held on. She pulled and pulled. He held on tighter and tighter. "*Nooooooo*," he wailed.

"You're *afraid* to come out," Sophie said.

"Am not."

"Are too."

"Not."

"Too."

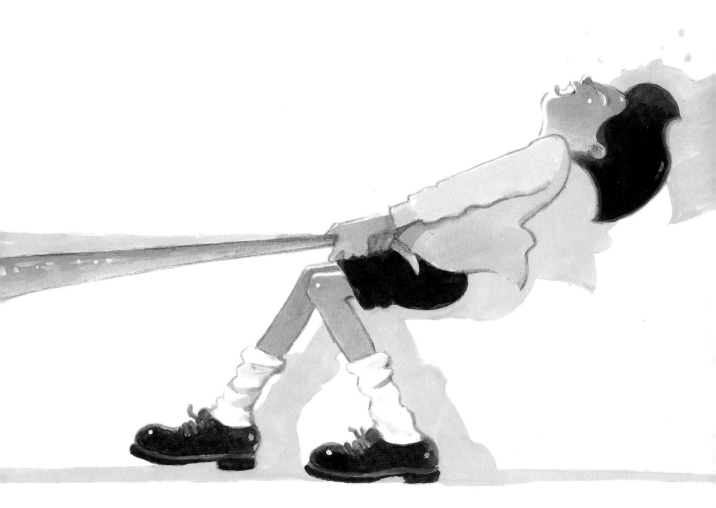

"*I*'m a *sea monster*," he said. "I'm not afraid of things. *Things* are afraid of *me*."

"I'm not," said Sophie.

The sea monster made a gargling monster noise from under the bed.

"Go eat a sock," said Sophie.

All was quiet for a while. Then Sophie asked, "So why do you stay under the bed?"

"Well," the sea monster said, "it might be too hot out there. Or too cold. And there are leopards. And snapping turtles and bicycles. And anteaters. What if the moon falls on my head? What's holding that thing up anyway?" He looked out the window. "But most of all," he said, "there are sea monsters."

"*You're* a sea monster," she said.

"Exactly," he said.

"Aren't you supposed to be in the sea?" Sophie asked.

"I'm afraid of water," he said. "Also sharks, whales and eels."

The next night, Sophie sat on her bed. "Do you want to read a book with me?" she asked.

"No," said the sea monster from under the bed.

"Once upon a time . . ." Sophie began.

After a few minutes, the sea monster came out. He looked around the room, then finally sat down and looked at the pictures.

*O*n Monday, they went outside.

On Tuesday, they took a bath.

On Wednesday, they rode bicycles to the museum and looked at dinosaurs and broken dishes. They tasted kidney beans for the first time.

"*Aaack,*" yelled the sea monster.

"*Aaack,*" said Sophie.

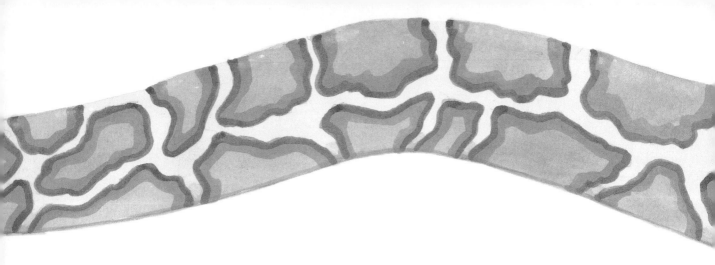

On Thursday, they went to the zoo and looked at anteaters and leopards and snapping turtles. The zookeeper brought out a python and let everyone touch it.

"Yikes," Sophie said as she patted the snake, which wasn't slimy like she thought it would be.

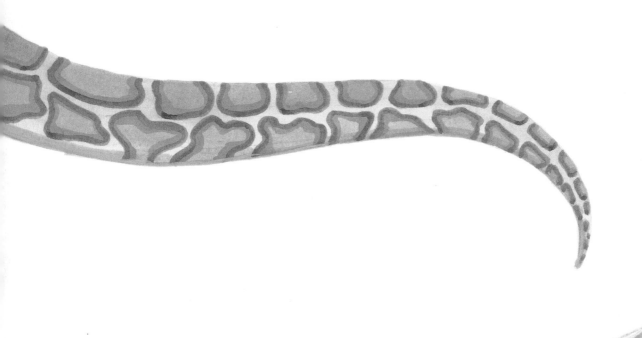

That night, they went outside to look at the moon, which was shining like a yellow balloon right above them. They went down to the beach and danced the moondance. They shook and spun and dipped and jived like crazy, and sang,

Oh let that big old moon
fall down from the sky
and land on all our homework
like a pumpkin pie.

We know it's big and round
and held up with a string
but we are wild and daring
so we'll just dance and sing.